Simon and his boxes

Gilles Tibo

Tundra Books

My name is Simon and I love boxes.

When I find a great big box
I build a house and move inside.

I find boxes for my animal friends,
I want everyone to have a house.

But they won't stay in them.

I build tall houses for the birds.

But they just look and fly away.

I ride to the river on my horse.

I put out houses for the fish.

They jump in...
But jump right out.

I build the biggest city ever.

But no one even comes to look.

I go to a tree to ask the Robot,
"Why won't animals come to my city?"

"Maybe they can't find it," said the Robot.

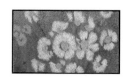

Marlene and I build a train.

We ride through the fields and into the forest.

We invite the animals to come to the city.

But they all get scared and run away.

I go to the cave to ask Jack-in-the-Box,
"Why won't animals live in my houses?"

"I like boxes and you like boxes," said Jack.
"I could not live any place else.
But the animals already have homes of their own.
Find something else to do with boxes."

And I did.

To Sarah

© **1992, Gilles Tibo**

Published in Canada by Tundra Books, Montreal, Quebec H3Z 2N2

Published in the United States by Tundra Books of Northern New York, Plattsburgh, N.Y. 12901

Distributed in the United Kingdom by Ragged Bears Ltd., Andover, Hampshire SP11 9HX

Library of Congress Catalog Number: 92-80416

Canadian Cataloging in Publication Data

Tibo, Gilles, 1951-.
     Simon and his boxes

ISBN 0-88776-287-5 (hardcover) 10 9 8 7 6 5 4 3 2 1
ISBN 0-88776-345-6 (paperback) 10 9 8 7 6 5 4 3 2 1

[Issued also in French under title: *Simon et la ville de carton* ISBN 0-88776-346-4]

     I. Title. II. Title: Simon et la ville de carton. English.

PS8589.I26S4613 1992   jC843'.54   C92-090174-3

Printed in Hong Kong by South China Printing Co. Ltd.